E   Ziefert, Harriet.
Zie   Train song

DATE DUE

MAR 28		
MAY 07		
OCT 22	TreyC	
APR 16		
OCT 25	MC	
FEB 13	SS	
GAYLORD		PRINTED IN U.S.A.

TRAIN SONG

by **Harriet Ziefert**

paintings by **Donald Saaf**

ORCHARD BOOKS • NEW YORK

For Nate—H.Z.

For Ole—D.S.

Orchard Books, A Grolier Company, 95 Madison Avenue, New York, NY 10016

Printed in China for Harriet Ziefert, Inc.
The text of this book is set in 24 point Antique Olive Roman.
The illustrations are gouache.

10 9 8 7 6 5 4 3 2 1

Library of Congress Cataloging-in-Publication Data
Ziefert, Harriet.
Train song / by Harriet Ziefert ; illustrated by Donald Saaf.
    p.   cm.
Summary: A young boy watches a freight train go by on its daily run.
ISBN 0-531-30204-0 (trade)
[1. Railroads—Trains Fiction. 2. Stories in rhyme.] I. Saaf, Donald, ill. II. Title.
PZ8.3.Z47Tr   2000
[E]—dc21   99-32219

Chug-a-chug-chug and clickety-clack . . .
Freight train must be coming back.

Freight train whistles long and loud.
Engineer is mighty proud.

Chug-a-chug-chug and clickety-clack . . .
Steam is white and the engine's black.

Chug-a-chug-chug and clickety-clack . . .
Freight train never leaves the track.

Little black engine sure can pull.
Even when her cars are full.

All those cars chug-a-chug along.
Freight train sings a lively song.

A small boy stands and waves his arms.
Freight train passes towns and farms.

Three spotted cows in the cattle car
Never thought they'd travel so far.

Ducks and geese and roosters and hens.
Can you count all sixteen pens?

See that car piled high with logs.
Other one carries a load of hogs.

Three big hogs go rolling along.
They all listen to the freight train song.

Tank car has a shiny side.
Don't you wonder what's inside?

Watch that engine chug-a-chug along.
Freight train sings a noisy song.

Hear her whistle and see her run
Through the tunnel and into the sun.

Clickety-clack and don't look back.
Trainman gotta watch that track.

Down the hill and put on the brake.
Engineer can't make a mistake!

Around the bend and up the grade...
Strongest engine ever made.

Freight train's chugging down the line.
Red caboose is pulled behind.

Watch the smoke that fills the sky,
As that train goes rolling by.

Chug-a-chug-chug and clickety-clack . . .
Steam is white and the engine's black.

Chug-a-chug-chug and clickety-clack...
Freight train never leaves the track.

Tomorrow when it's almost ten,
Freight train will be back again.